Dear Parents:

Congratulations! Your child is taking the first steps on an exciting journey. The destination? Independent reading!

STEP INTO READING® will help your child get there. The program offers five steps to reading success. Each step includes fun stories and colorful art or photographs. In addition to original fiction and books with favorite characters, there are Step into Reading Non-Fiction Readers, Phonics Readers and Boxed Sets, Sticker Readers, and Comic Readers—a complete literacy program with something to interest every child.

Learning to Read, Step by Step!

Ready to Read Preschool–Kindergarten
• big type and easy words • rhyme and rhythm • picture clues
For children who know the alphabet and are eager to begin reading.

Reading with Help Preschool–Grade 1
• basic vocabulary • short sentences • simple stories
For children who recognize familiar words and sound out new words with help.

Reading on Your Own Grades 1–3
• engaging characters • easy-to-follow plots • popular topics
For children who are ready to read on their own.

Reading Paragraphs Grades 2–3
• challenging vocabulary • short paragraphs • exciting stories
For newly independent readers who read simple sentences with confidence.

Ready for Chapters Grades 2–4
• chapters • longer paragraphs • full-color art
For children who want to take the plunge into chapter books but still like colorful pictures.

STEP INTO READING® is designed to give every child a successful reading experience. The grade levels are only guides; children will progress through the steps at their own speed, developing confidence in their reading. The F&P Text Level on the back cover serves as another tool to help you choose the right book for your child.

Remember, a lifetime love of reading starts with a single step!

For my granddaughter Asma Jama,
who reminds me of Rabia!
—R.K.

To Alesha, let's wear henna on our
hands together one day.
—D.R.

Text copyright © 2024 by Rukhsana Khan
Cover art and interior illustrations copyright © 2024 by Debby Rahmalia

All rights reserved. Published in the United States by Random House Children's Books, a division of Penguin Random House LLC, New York.

Step into Reading, Random House, and the Random House colophon are registered trademarks of Penguin Random House LLC.

Visit us on the Web!
rhcbooks.com

Educators and librarians, for a variety of teaching tools, visit us at RHTeachersLibrarians.com

Library of Congress Cataloging-in-Publication Data
Names: Khan, Rukhsana, author. | Rahmalia, Debby, illustrator.
Title: Rabia's Eid / by Rukhsana Khan ; illustrated by Debby Rahmalia.
Description: First edition. | New York : Random House, [2024] | Series: Step into reading | Audience: Ages 4–6. | Summary: Rabia tries fasting for the first time on Eid al-Fitr, the last day of Ramadan.
Identifiers: LCCN 2022060115 (print) | LCCN 2022060116 (ebook) |
ISBN 978-0-593-70681-7 (trade paperback) | ISBN 978-0-593-70682-4 (library binding) |
ISBN 978-0-593-70683-1 (ebook)
Subjects: CYAC: Eid al-Fitr—Fiction. | Fasts and feasts—Fiction. | Muslims—Fiction. |
LCGFT: Readers (Publications)
Classification: LCC PZ7.K52654 Rab 2024 (print) | LCC PZ7.K52654 (ebook) | DDC [Fic]—dc23

Printed in the United States of America
10 9 8 7 6 5 4 3 2 1
First Edition

This book has been officially leveled by using the F&P Text Level Gradient™ Leveling System.

Rabia's Eid

by Rukhsana Khan

illustrated by Debby Rahmalia

Random House 🏠 New York

It was still dark.
Rabia heard Mom
come in.

"Wake up, Maryam,"
said Mom.
"It is the last day of
Ramadan."

Rabia sat up in her bed.
"I want to fast, too,"
said Rabia.

"You are too little,"
said Maryam.
"Go back to sleep, Rabia,"
said Mom.

But Rabia followed them
into the kitchen.
Dad was eating cereal,
getting ready to fast.

"Why are you up, Rabia?"
he asked.
"She wants to fast, too,"
said Maryam.
"But it is hard not to
eat all day."

"Let her try a half day,"
said Dad.

Rabia clapped her hands.

So Rabia ate her cereal
and drank some water.

Soon it was time
to start fasting.

Rabia said the prayer
with her family.
She felt so grown up.

At first,
fasting was easy.
She was not very hungry
or thirsty.

But by lunchtime,
her tummy growled
and her mouth was dry.

Rabia was ready to
break her fast.
"Good job," said Maryam.
"Good job," said Mom.
"We are proud of you."

Rabia ate
a cheese and tomato
sandwich.
It tasted extra good!

When the sun set,
the rest of the family
was ready
to break their fast.

Like Mom, Dad,
and Maryam,
Rabia picked up a date.

They said a prayer.

Then they ate their dates.
Mmm, so sweet!

"Now comes the fun!"
said Mom.
She drew flower designs
on their hands
with henna paste.

"Do not touch anything till the henna is dry," said Mom.

"Okay," said Rabia.

When the henna
was dry,
the designs did not
wash off.

The designs were
so pretty!

At bedtime,
Rabia and Maryam
laid out their new
Eid clothes.

In the morning,
the girls sparkled
in their matching
dresses!

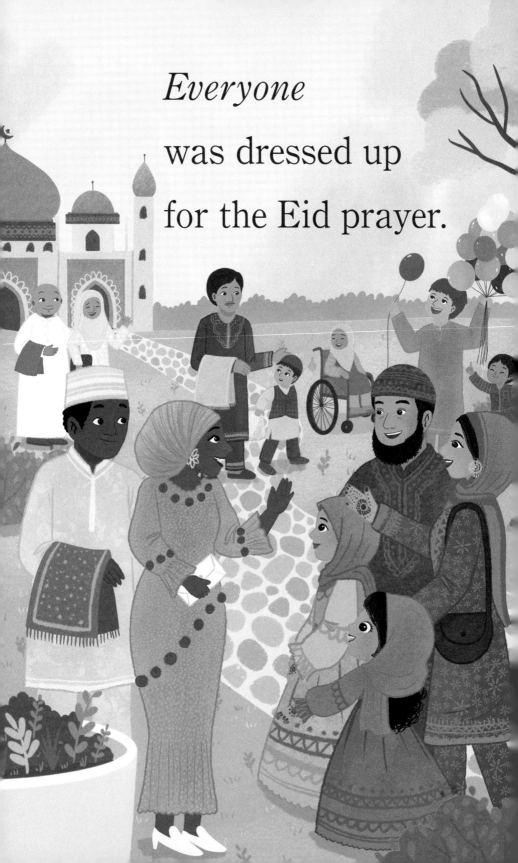

Everyone was dressed up for the Eid prayer.

Dad put money in
Rabia's hand.

"What is this for?"
asked Rabia.
"It is for the poor,"
said Dad.

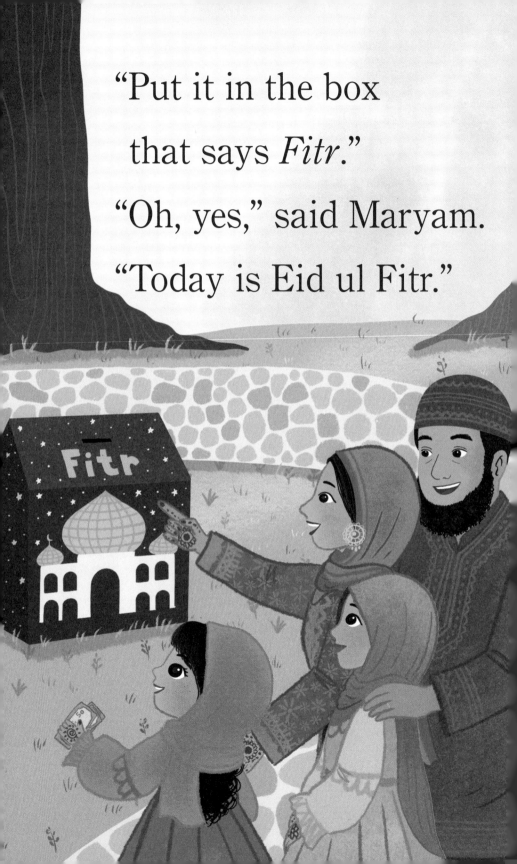

"Put it in the box
that says *Fitr*."
"Oh, yes," said Maryam.
"Today is Eid ul Fitr."

Rabia looked at the
money in her hand.

Then she looked at
the big crowd of people.

"Do we *all* give Fitr?"
she asked.

"Yes, everyone except
the poor!" said Mom.

Rabia smiled
as she tucked
the money into the box.

Now she knew others
would have an Eid
as happy as hers!